TITCHY WITCH

AND THE DISAPPEARING BABY

ROSE IMPEY ★ KATHARINE McEWEN

ORCHARD

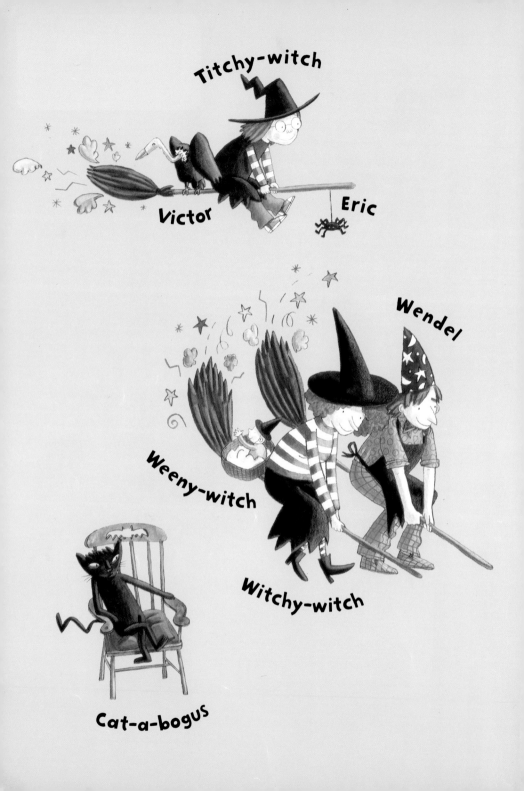

Titchy-witch

Victor

Eric

Wendel

Weeny-witch

Witchy-witch

Cat-a-bogus

Titchy-witch was a happy little witch… while the baby was inside Mum's tummy.

But then one day Weeny-witch
came out.

It was magic, but not the kind
of magic Titchy-witch liked.
Being a titchy big sister was
no fun at all.

Titchy-witch didn't think
much of weeny witches.
They made too much work.

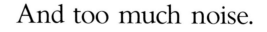

And too much noise.

8

And *terrible* weeny witchy smells.

Titchy-witch wanted Mum
to play with *her*.

And feed *her* mashed beetles
and banana.

And cuddle *her* and sing:
"This little witch went
a-haunting."

But now Witchy-witch was
always busy with the baby.

And there were always visitors
standing round the cradle,
oohing-and-aahing.

"Isn't she bewitching!" they said.

"Oh, yes," said Witchy-witch.

"Oh, yuck!" said Titchy-witch.

When Titchy-witch went to find
Dad, he was busy too. Wendel
was always in his workshop,
testing spells for his
new book.

DO NOT
DISTURB
—
WIZARD
AT WORK

Even her mum's cat, Cat-a-bogus, was too busy with weeny witch business. He twitched his tail and disappeared.

Titchy-witch tried to disappear too.

But she wasn't very good
at spells yet.

Sometimes she practised on
Victor...

...or Eric.

Luckily her spells didn't last very
long.

One day the baby was crying,
even more than usual.
Mum said she was
getting a new fang.

When Mum went for a rest she left
Titchy-witch to watch the baby.
The noise was giving her a
headache.

Titchy-witch peeped into the cradle.
Her nose began to twitch.
Her fingers began to wiggle.

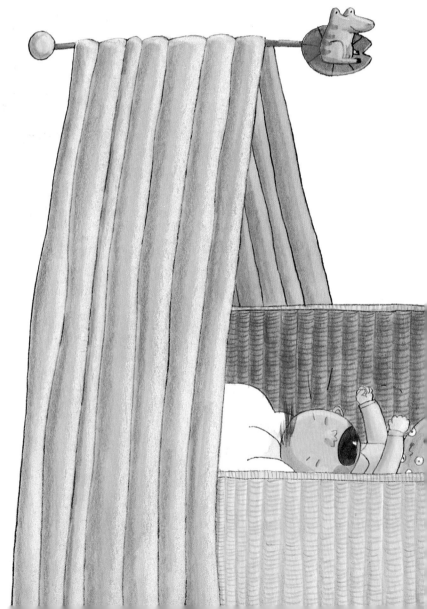

Suddenly a spell *popped into* her head and the magic words just *popped out.*

"Fizzy-fuzzy rabbit's ear, Make this baby disappear!"

It was quiet now!
Weeny-witch hadn't exactly
disappeared.

But the bit that was crying had.

Titchy-witch looked for the baby's head...

...but she couldn't find it anywhere.
Just then, along
came more trouble.

Cat-a-bogus thought he was
the boss of the house. He twitched
his tail crossly.
"What's going on?" he asked.

Titchy-witch was thinking up
a good story.
But the cat said, "And I want
no taradiddles."
So Titchy-witch told the truth.

The cat growled. Little witches and little spells usually added up to big trouble.

"And who will have to put
it right?" he asked.

"You will," said Titchy-witch,
sadly.

She hoped the cat would put
it right, now, this minute. She didn't
like having a baby sister without
a head.

Cat-a-bogus
knew lots
of magic and
he liked
to show off.
He stretched
very tall
and purred
some magic
words under
his breath.

"Arragon,
Tarragon,
Sim-sala-bim."

Weeny-witch's head reappeared,
and she wasn't
crying now.

In fact, she seemed to have enjoyed
her trip.

When the baby looked up at her
and gurgled, it gave Titchy-witch
a nice feeling in her tummy.
Like tiny bats flying about inside.

No, she thought, weeny witch
sisters aren't so bad, after all.

TITCHY WITCH

BY ROSE IMPEY   ILLUSTRATED BY KATHARINE McEWEN

Enjoy a little more magic with all the Titchy-witch tales:

Orchard Books are available from all good
bookshops, or can be ordered from our website:
www.orchardbooks.co.uk
or telephone 01235 827702, or fax 01235 827703.

Prices and availability are subject to change.